£3.75

My Little Pony

ANNUAL 1988

CONTENTS

Copyright © 1987 Hasbro Industries (UK) Limited.
All rights reserved.
Published in Great Britain by
World International Publishing Limited,
An Egmont Company,
Egmont House, P.O. Box 111, Great Ducie Street,
Manchester M60 3BL.
Printed in Great Britain.
SBN 7235 6804 9

Stories by Pat Posner

A HAZARDOUS TIME IN PONY LAND

"Spike! Spike! Where are you?" shouted Baby Lucky. "Come up to the battlements and look through the telescope. Hurry up, there's something to see."

"What?" Spike shouted back. "What is there to see? I can't come up now, I'm packing my cases."

"Heavy hooves," muttered Baby Lucky. "I'd forgotten about Spike's holiday. I'm really going to miss him, he'll be in the Land of Dragons for two days."

Just then, Wind Whistler flew over the castle turrets.

"Hello, Baby Lucky," she called. "Have you looked through the telescope this morning? Have you seen the..."

"Seen what? What is there to see?" roared Spike, running up to join his friend. "Why didn't you answer me, Baby Lucky? I haven't got time to keep running up here. Don't land there, Wind Whistler, I want to look through the telescope and I'm in a hurry. I'm going on holiday today, you know."

Wind Whistler laughed and landed right in front of the little

said Baby Lucky. "You can see the bubbles without using it."

"Fancy calling me up here just to see bubbles," snorted Spike. "What a waste of time. I'm going to finish packing." And the little dragon hurried away. Baby Lucky looked sadly after his friend.

"Don't look so sad," said Wind Whistler, gently. "Spike always gets a bit cross before he goes to the Land of Dragons. His great-grand-father sends a list of things he wants Spike to take with him, and Spike worries in case he forgets anything. He doesn't mean to be cross and bossy."

"I know that," replied Baby Lucky. "Spike's my best friend, he never gets cross with me. I'm going to miss him, that's why I feel sad."

"You won't have time to miss him," said Wind Whistler. "Have you forgotten what the coloured bubbles mean? They're an invitation from Sprinkles and Duck Soup."

"An invitation to what?" asked Baby Lucky.

"To a party at the Waterfall," replied Wind Whistler. "Go and get ready

dragon. "You are a bossy thing today, Spike," said Wind Whistler. "There's no reason for you to look through the telescope, whatever there is to see won't concern you. You won't be here for it."

"Frantic feet! What won't I be here for?" demanded Spike. "Do move over, Wind Whistler, and let me look through the telescope."

Suddenly, dozens of red, green, blue, yellow and orange bubbles floated merrily around Dream Castle. "You don't need to look through the telescope now,"

then come to Lullaby Nursery, I'll meet you there."

"No, I'll meet you at the Waterfall later," said Baby Lucky. "I'm going to see if Spike needs any help with his packing. I've got a good memory, I'll help him remember everything for his great-grandfather."

Wind Whistler smiled as the baby pony hurried away to help Spike. And I'll make sure that he doesn't miss Spike too much, she thought, I'll have to think of some interesting games for him to play at Sprinkles' party. I'll ask Baby Tiddly Winks to think of some as well, she knows lots of games. I'd better hurry to the nursery and help the baby ponies get ready.

Spike *was* pleased to see Baby Lucky. "I'm sorry I was so cross," said the little dragon. "It's just that I've got such a lot to remember."

"I know, Wind Whistler told me about your great-grandfather's list," said Baby Lucky. "I've come to see if I can help you. After all, it was your great-grandfather who gave you the lucky birthday that you share with me, so it will be nice for me to do something for him."

The lucky birthday was an extra birthday awarded to a dragon once every hundred years. When Spike had been awarded the birthday by his

great-grandfather, he'd had to find somebody to share the birthday. He'd found Baby Lucky so now they both shared the birthday that would make them lucky forever.

"I know what you can do," said Spike. "Will you go and find Majesty and ask her if she's got any spare lavender bags? Great-grandfather likes to put them in with his best uniforms to make them smell nice."

"What sort of uniforms does he wear, and why does he wear them?" asked Baby Lucky. Spike explained that

the uniforms were worn every week for the Dragons' Parade. "Oh, I do wish I could come with you," sighed Baby Lucky. "I'd love to see the parade."

"Why don't you come with me?" shouted Spike. "I'm sure great-grandfather would like to meet you. Like you said, we do share the lucky birthday he awarded me."

"I'll ask Majesty if I can, when I ask her about the lavender bags," said Baby Lucky, wriggling with excitement.

"No, don't ask her," said Spike naughtily. "She might say no. We'll just leave her a note to say that you've gone with me. And I've got some lavender bags somewhere, we'll take those with us instead of asking Majesty for some."

"Shh!" warned Baby Lucky, who had very sharp ears, "I can hear someone coming. I think it's Majesty."

"Hide behind the curtain," whispered Spike urgently. "If Majesty sees you she'll know you're excited about something. And don't wriggle," he added, as he pulled the curtain straight.

Spike hurried back to his cases and by the time Majesty came in he looked very busy. "I've brought you some lavender bags," said Majesty, passing a brightly wrapped package to the little dragon. "They're a present for your great-grandfather, I know he likes them."

"Oh, thank you, Majesty," said Spike. "We were just talking about lavender bags when..." Spike suddenly stopped talking. He'd nearly mentioned Baby Lucky! It was a good job that Majesty wasn't really listening to Spike. She had just noticed how untidily the little dragon

had packed his cases.

"You'd better take everything out and start all over again," she said. "I'll help you but we mustn't take long, Sprinkles is having a party and I promised to take some soap down to the Waterfall. One of the party games is a bubble blowing competition." Majesty worked quickly and before long she'd re-packed one of Spike's cases.

"I'll do the second one," said Spike, as he noticed the curtain that Baby Lucky was hiding behind starting to move. "I'll do it neatly this time, I promise."

"All right," agreed Majesty. "Have a nice holiday and I'll see you in two days. I'll fetch Baby Lucky, he can help me carry the soap to Sprinkles. You don't know where he is, do you?"

"He was here just before you came in," replied Spike, truthfully.

"Oh, well, he's probably in the courtyard," said Majesty, as she left the room.

"I didn't tell a fib," said Spike when Majesty had gone. "You were here just before she came in."

"You just didn't tell her I was still here," said Baby Lucky. "I'm glad I didn't have to stay behind the curtain any longer, I was starting to wriggle."

"I'll finish packing and you go and write a note for Majesty," ordered Spike. "Be as quick as you can in case she comes back."

Spike hummed happily to himself while he finished packing. He was really pleased that his friend was going to the Land of Dragons with him. I hope Majesty won't be too cross, he thought, but we are leaving her a note. She will know where Baby Lucky is. We'll have to go through the secret passage that runs under the courtyard and comes out at the cave in Windy Cliffs. None of the little ponies will see us then. I'll take the magic moonstone that North Star gave me. It will light up the passage, it's ever so dark down there.

So a few minutes later, the two friends set off. Baby Lucky felt very excited, he'd never been through the secret passage before. "We'll have to be very quiet at first," whispered Spike. "The entrance is right under the kitchen window."

"Are you sure Majesty isn't in the garden?" Baby Lucky whispered back.

"I'm sure," hissed Spike. "She'll either be round the other side in the courtyard, or in the kitchen. That's why we've got to be very quiet. Now come on and stop asking questions." Keeping close against the castle walls, Baby Lucky crept behind the little dragon. He was so busy looking down at his hooves, to make sure they didn't make a noise, that he nearly fell over Spike when he stopped by the kitchen window.

Spike dropped his cases and they both held their breath in case anyone had heard the thud. "It's all right," whispered Spike, "but just stand back a bit while I move this stone." The stone was well hidden in a patch of stinging nettles and Baby Lucky

thought what a good job it was that Spike's skin was so tough and scaly.

"Right," puffed Spike, as the large cobblestone slid back. "Jump down into the hole and wait for me. Can you manage one of my cases?" Baby Lucky nodded, he was too excited to even whisper.

The little dragon waited until he heard Baby Lucky land with a soft thud then he jumped into the hole. "Now I'll have to pull that handle down," he told Baby Lucky, and he pointed to a huge handle fixed in the stone above him.

"It's too high for you," whispered the baby pony.

"Even I can't reach it and I'm much taller than you."

Spike opened the case that he was carrying and took the magic moonstone out. "Look," he said, and the glow from the moonstone shone onto some footholds that were carved in the rocky wall. "That's how I reach the handle, I have to climb up. You shine the moonstone onto the right places, Baby Lucky."

The little dragon was a very good climber and he soon reached the handle. But no matter how hard he pulled he just couldn't make it move. "I'll have to jump up and swing on it," he muttered at last.

Baby Lucky nearly dropped the moonstone when he saw what his friend was doing.

"I still can't move it," Spike called softly. "I'm going to turn upside down and swing by my legs. They're stronger than my arms." Baby Lucky held the moonstone very tightly and shone it onto the handle. His eyes grew enormous as he watched Spike wriggling over the top of the handle. He moaned softly to himself when it looked as if Spike's legs were slipping off the handle.

"It's all right," panted Spike. "I'm safe." And as he swung himself backwards and forwards the cobblestone slid back into place over the entrance. Then something terrible happened!

There was a strange grating noise and suddenly the handle

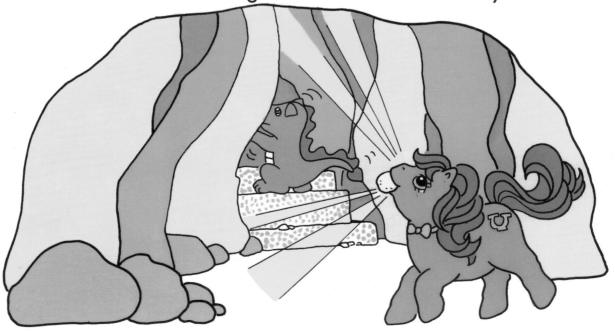

came away from the wall. Poor Spike was still clinging to it with his legs. "Dismal dragons!" he wailed as he hurtled downwards. Baby Lucky didn't have time to move and the little dragon landed right on top of him.

"Ouch. I'm lying on top of the moonstone!" howled Baby Lucky. "Happy-go-Lucky, I wish..."

"Oh, no," groaned Spike. "When will you learn to remember what happens when you say those words?" And almost before Spike had finished speaking, the moonstone started to grow and grow.

"I don't know the words to stop it growing!" shouted Baby Lucky. "Move, Spike, quickly..."

But it was too late. The moonstone was now the size of a huge rock. And the baby pony and the little dragon were trapped between it and the wall of the tunnel. They couldn't climb over, under or around it.

"What are we going to do now?" sighed Spike. "Nobody knows we're here. They won't even start looking for us. They'll all think we're in

the Land of Dragons."

"We'll be trapped here for ever and ever," moaned Baby Lucky. "We'll starve to..."

"Don't be so mournful. Eat the moonstone. That's what I've been doing ever since I got trapped inside it."

"Who was that?" asked Spike and Baby Lucky together. "Who spoke to us?"

13

"I did, I did. Oh, it's so nice to be out of the moonstone." A tiny little moonmouse jumped out of the huge moonstone. "Well, don't just stand there staring at me," commanded the moonmouse. "Start eating the moonstone. It tastes quite nice when you get used to it."

"But it will take ages to eat it all," said Baby Lucky. "We'll still be trapped for ever and ever."

"No we won't!" shouted

Spike, starting to gnaw at the moonstone. "We'll only have to make a tiny space for the moonmouse to squeeze through, then he can go along the passage to the cave. He'll easily find his way to the Waterfall from Windy Cliffs. Come on, Baby Lucky! Eat some moonstone."

"Ugh! It tastes horrible," whimpered Baby Lucky. "Poor, poor Baby Lucky feels sick."

"No you don't," said Spike. "Keep eating. We'll have made a space in a minute."

"Hurry up! Hurry up!" squeaked the moonmouse. "Now I'm out of the moonstone I can't wait to run around outside. I'll go to your Waterfall, tell the little ponies where you are, then I'm going to run all over Pony Land."

It didn't really take long for Spike and Baby Lucky to eat away enough moonstone. But to the baby pony it seemed as if he'd been eating moonstone for days and days.

However, at last there was a space big enough for the moonmouse to scramble through. "I'll see you when I've finished exploring Pony

Land," called the moonmouse. "And don't worry, I'll send somebody to rescue you, I promise."

Spike and Baby Lucky were so tired and so full of moonstone that they fell asleep. And that's how Majesty found them after she'd twirled her magic horn and returned the moonstone to its proper size!

But Spike and the baby pony still had a journey to make. Not even Majesty's magic could repair the handle that had fallen from the roof of the tunnel. So they couldn't go back the way they'd come.

They had to walk right through the passage to the cave, then all the way from Windy Cliffs to Dream Castle.

Spike and Baby Lucky didn't have a holiday in the Land of Dragons after all. And Baby Lucky had to promise Majesty that he'd never, ever go anywhere without first asking her if he could.

But they did make a new friend. After the moonmouse had finished exploring Pony Land he went to live in Dream Castle. The little dragon, the baby pony and the tiny moonmouse were to have many adventures together!

A TRAIN RIDE THROUGH PONY LAND

"Happy-go-Lucky!" When Baby Lucky says the magic words his toy train just grows and grows. Then the little ponies clamber inside and go for a train ride through Pony Land.

Here is Snapdragon Valley — one of Spike's favourite places. If you look carefully you'll see a snapdragon flower that looks like Spike.

Confetti and Parasol love visiting Paper Place. The Paper Pixies are their special friends. It's very windy today and the Paper Birds are staying in the trees so they don't get blown away. Can you see six Paper Birds?

The baby ponies shout with glee when they arrive at the Cave of Echoes. Baby Shady wants to wear her magic sunglasses then she might be able to see the echo! But somebody else wants to see the echo as well. Who is hiding the magic sunglasses?

Time for ice-skates and sledges now. It's always snowy in Winter Wonderland. Just look at all the snow houses. Can you see snow people peeping out of the windows?

Here's Fantasy Forest. North Star has to use her magic compass to guide the little ponies through here. Just as they think they are in one place the scenery changes and they find themselves somewhere else. Even the sun seems to be in the wrong place, doesn't it?

SHADY'S SECRET

Shady's friends often thought she was joking when she described what she could see through her special sunglasses.

So, one night, when Shady saw a strange wall with many little doors set in it, she decided to keep it a secret. "I know where the wall is," Shady whispered to herself. "I can see a parasol-shaped tree and there's only one tree like that in Pony Land."

It was a dark night but that didn't matter. When Shady wore her sunglasses it seemed like daytime to her.

The little pony was on her way to Sleepy Hollow. It was a strange place. Few ponies went there.

Shady felt quite tired by the time she reached Sleepy Hollow. Tired but excited! The wall looked even bigger now she was here. Slowly, she walked around it, wondering which door to go through.

The little pony smiled as she passed a door shaped like a clown. She was almost sure she'd seen the clown's nose move.

"Oh, I don't like this door," shuddered Shady, as a luminous face bared its teeth and grinned horribly at her.

The horrible face had frightened Shady. She decided to go in the very next door she came to. Strangely, the next door was open. The little pony hurried through it. "I'm at a fair!" exclaimed Shady. "There's a merry-go-round and..."

Shady took her sunglasses off and stared at the merry-go-round. "All the ponies look like me," she said.

"Are you the pony who got off the merry-go-round and took some of our friends away?" asked a green goblin.

"She is. She must be." Shady was suddenly surrounded by all sorts of angrily chattering pixie folk.

"Of course I'm not!" said Shady. "I live in Dream Valley. I've never seen this place before."

"How did you get here, then?" shouted a long-bearded gnome. "I saw the wall with all its different doors through my sunglasses," explained Shady. "Which different doors? There's only one door," said the gnome, snatching Shady's sunglasses and putting them on himself.

"Nervous gnomes! The little pony's right. I can see other doors!" cried the gnome. "And I can see...I can see...oh..."

Shady took her sunglasses back, then looked through them herself. "Heavy hooves, your friends are next door!"

Shady shuddered. "The pony from the merry-go-round isn't there," she said. "Are you *sure* you're not the one?" asked a goblin.

"I'm a real little pony!" Shady tossed her mane. "The ponies on the merry-go-round are just toys. They can't walk or talk."

"One walked off with our friends," said the goblin. "Did you see it walk off?" asked Shady angrily. "Did you?"

The pixie folk chattered to each other. "Nobody saw the pony walk off," admitted the goblin. "Oh, please help us."

"We'll have to go next door," said Shady. "And once we're in there we'll have to move very fast." "We'll go in my train!" shouted the driver. "I'll make it puff out lots of smoke so nobody can see us." "We won't be able to see anybody either!" said a goblin. "I will," stated Shady.

The brave little pony led the way out of one door and up to the other. The face leered at her, but she opened the door.

There were wailing noises and clouds of smoke puffed from the train. Shady was terrified!

But she could see the pixie folk. "This time I'll bring good luck to somebody," muttered the little pony determinedly. Shady often thought she brought bad luck. "Jump onto my back!" she cried urgently. "No, no," moaned the pixie folk. "The faces won't let us."

Just then, the hideous faces were covered by clouds of smoke. "Our fairground train is here!" shouted a pixie.

"Come on! Jump up before all the smoke disappears," begged Shady. One by one, the pixie folk obeyed her.

"Hold tight, you're going home," laughed Shady, and she galloped back the way she'd come. The train followed behind, bellowing smoke.

Shady galloped in through the open door. To her amazement, she found herself back inside Dream Castle!

"Come on, Shady. Don't you want to come to the Pixie Fairground?" asked Posey, impatiently. Shady sighed and took her sunglasses off. "All right," she said. "Let's go." The little ponies enjoyed the fair. "The toy merry-go-round ponies look just like Shady," they laughed.

24

FIREBALL'S FLAPDOODLE

One morning Baby Lucky was woken up by the sound of hooves thundering across the courtyard. As he hurried across to the window to see what all the noise was about a bright flash lit up the room. "Oh, it's the mountain boy ponies," said Baby Lucky. "They must be going on one of their outings."

"Yes, they are," said Majesty, who had just come into the room. "I asked Lightning to wake me up before they went. That's why he made that bright flash."

"It must be very early, it's not properly light yet," said Baby Lucky. "Why did you want them to wake you?"

"Silky, the little spider, spent all night making this silver thread," explained Majesty. "It's for Dame Dorcas, she's weaving some blankets for Prince High and Mighty's wedding present."

"Are the mountain ponies taking the silver thread to Dame Dorcas?" asked Baby Lucky. "Can I go with them? I like visiting Dame Dorcas, she lets me play games with her spinning wheel."

"Well, you take this thread

to Fireball," suggested Majesty, "and ask him if you can join them. But you mustn't be too disappointed if he won't let you."

So Baby Lucky ran through Dream Castle and outside into the courtyard. "Have you brought the silver thread?" demanded Fireball. "Lightning was just about to make another flash, we thought Majesty hadn't heard or seen us."

"Yes, it's here," replied Baby Lucky, giving the small package to Fireball. "Please can I come with you?"

"Don't be silly, of course you can't," said Fireball. "This outing is for boy ponies only."

"But I'm a boy pony, too," said Baby Lucky. "It's not fair. Why can't I come?"

"Because," Fireball spoke impatiently, "you're a baby boy. The outing's for big boy ponies. The six of us are going to visit our friend the magician after we've delivered the silver thread."

"The magician who lives in Misty Mountain?" asked Baby Lucky. "Oh, please let me come. You know I like it in Misty Mountain."

"It's too far for baby ponies like you!" scoffed Tornado.

"I know it's a long way," admitted Baby Lucky. "But we needn't come back today. We could go to Misty Mountain first, then take the thread to Dame Dorcas and stay with her overnight. We..."

"Flapdoodle!" snorted Fireball. "We want to be back here by teatime. It's the all-night jumping marathon tonight and it starts at six o'clock."

"I'm fed up of being a baby pony!" shouted Baby Lucky. "I can't go in for the jumping marathon, either. Anyway, what does flapdoodle mean?" he added. "You're always saying it."

"It means nonsense," stated Fireball. "And that's what you are. A great big flapdoodle. Now, it's time for us to go. I can't stay here flapdoodling with you any longer."

The big boy ponies hurried away and Baby Lucky watched sadly. Then he wandered around the courtyard wishing, not for the first time, that he was a big boy pony, too. "They have all the fun," he muttered crossly.

"I've come back to make something special for you. Something that will be fun." And suddenly Ice Crystal appeared. He had seen how upset Baby Lucky was and decided to do something about it.

"What are you doing here?" asked Baby Lucky. "You were with your big friends when they left."

"I told you," chuckled Ice Crystal. "I've come back to make something for you. I'm going to make some slides and you can hold an all-day sliding marathon while we're gone."

"That's a babyish sort of marathon," said Baby Lucky.

"It won't be," promised Ice Crystal. "I'll make very long slides for you. It will be ever so hard for any pony to reach the end of them without falling. And, of course, if they fall, they'll have to go back to the beginning of the slide and start all over again."

"Will it really be hard to do?" asked Baby Lucky, looking more cheerful. "They won't be...be...flapdoodle slides!"

"They certainly won't," said Ice Crystal. "Now you go and wake everyone up and tell them about your all-day marathon. By the time you come back there will be lots of slides here."

"Can I just watch while you make the first slide?" requested the baby pony. Ice

Crystal nodded and breathed in deeply. He held his breath for ten seconds, then breathed out slowly.

"You're right!" laughed Baby Lucky. "The slides won't be flapdoodles. That's going to be a *very* long slide." And the baby pony watched happily as Ice Crystal's breath turned to ice along the ground. "Merry manes! Thank you for thinking of the competition, Ice Crystal. But I hope you'll be able to catch the others up when you've finished making the slides."

"I'll be with them before you can say slide," chuckled Ice Crystal, "I can gallop very quickly, you know. Off you go, Baby Lucky, go and fetch your friends. I'll see you at teatime."

So Baby Lucky galloped away. "I'll only fetch the baby ponies, Spike, Twinkles, Brandy and Duck Soup," he said to himself. "Lemon Drop and the others will be too busy getting the jumps ready for their own marathon."

Spike had spent the night with Duck Soup and Sprinkles in a little cave behind the Waterfall. He hurried out when he heard Baby Lucky calling. "Hello, Baby Lucky!" shouted the little dragon. "You're up early. Come and see what I've done. I've been helping Sprinkles make the Bubble-Jump for tonight's marathon."

"I can't see anything," said Baby Lucky, peering into the pond beneath the Waterfall.

"Come into the cave and I'll show you," chuckled Spike. "Follow me and you won't get splashed. I know you don't like water!"

Baby Lucky followed Spike into the cave and stared in

amazement at the rows of huge shells. "The bubble liquid is inside the shells," explained Spike. "I helped to mix it up and pour it in. When it's time for the Bubble-Jump, Duck Soup, Sprinkles and Firefly will pour the liquid from the shells down the Waterfall. Then the pond will be covered in huge bubbles and the little ponies will have to jump over the pond without touching a bubble."

"That's clever," said Baby Lucky. "I've got something to show you, too. We are going to have a marathon of our own. An all-day sliding marathon. Ice Crystal's making some very long slides."

"Dandy ducks! Can I enter?" quacked Duck Soup. "It sounds like fun. Sliding is easy."

"Flapdoodle! Wait until you see the slides," giggled Baby Lucky. "Will you two go and get Twinkles and Brandy while I go to Lullaby Nursery? Meet me in the courtyard."

"Can I come and watch?" asked Kelpy, the little water sprite. "You can take me in this special shell house that Sprinkles made for me." Kelpy couldn't stay out of water for long, so Sprinkles had made her a little house that had a carpet of water.

"Of course you can come, you'll enjoy it," said Duck Soup. "I'll carry you there myself. Get into your shell house, Kelpy.''

Before long, all Baby Lucky's competitors were gathered in the courtyard. ''I'm not entering,'' mewed Twinkles. ''The slides are too long and my paws would freeze if I slid on them. I'll sit by Kelpy and watch.''

Kelpy giggled with delight. She'd got a new spell she wanted to try out and she knew Twinkles would help her. Kelpy's spells often went wrong. She was a young sprite, and could only make very easy spells work. But she knew this one would work. It would take quite a long time for she had to remember lots of words. That didn't matter though as the marathon was going on all day!

''You are a cowardy-cat,'' Brandy told Twinkles. ''Sliding is easy, your paws move so quickly they don't have time to freeze.'' Then Brandy barked in fright as his legs went from under him. ''Oh, well, maybe it isn't as easy as all that,'' he admitted. ''I'll have to go back to the beginning again.''

By the time four o'clock came nobody had manged to go from one end of a slide to the other, and Baby Lucky suggested that they all had a ten minute rest and something to eat.

"I'll make some ice-creams," offered Baby Lickety-Split. "And look, here's Majesty with some oat cakes."

"Do you want a go on a slide, Majesty?" asked Baby Lucky.

"I haven't got time," replied Majesty. "Gingerbread, Sweetie and I have been baking all day and we still haven't finished. We need lots of food for tonight's marathon. Gingerbread's organizing a Jump for the Cake competition."

"Your jumping marathon is going to be fun," said Baby Lucky. "But our sliding marathon is fun, too."

"The fun hasn't started yet," whispered Kelpy to Twinkles. "My spell is almost ready. You will remember to say the right words in the right place, won't you, Twinkles?"

"I will," promised Twinkles. "I hope Brandy is sliding when the spell works; he called me a cowardy-cat."

However, before the sliding marathon had started again, the mountain boy ponies returned. "Ice Crystal! Your slides are impossible," laughed the baby ponies.

"None of us have managed to slide all the way along one yet."

"I told you it would be ever so hard," said Ice Crystal, smiling at Baby Lucky.

"There's nothing to sliding," stated Tornado. "Watch me, I'll show you how to do it." But Tornado slipped over almost straight away.

"You put your hooves all wrong," laughed Sunburst. "That's why you fell."

"You shouldn't have taken such a long run," said Thundercloud.

"I think you should have held your tail up," said Lightning.

"Flapdoodle! You're all wrong," snorted Fireball. "He should have held his head on one side."

"You do it then," said Baby Lucky.

Fireball was halfway along a slide when Kelpy and Twinkles said the words to Kelpy's spell. Suddenly, all the separate slides joined up into one huge circular slide.

"It's worked!" shrieked Kelpy. "I've made a magic circle."

"It's whirling round and round," said Twinkles.

"The words you said made the whirly bit happen," said Kelpy.

"I can't stop going round!" shouted Fireball. "I can't stop sliding."

"How long does the spell work for?" giggled Twinkles. "Oh, I do wish Brandy had been on the slide when it worked."

"It lasts for half an hour," said Kelpy. "It's good, isn't it?"

"It's a...a...flapdoodle slide!" chortled Baby Lucky.

Kelpy was quite right. The spell did last for half an hour. Poor Fireball was very dizzy when the circular slide turned back into separate slides. "I don't think I can take part in the all-night jumping marathon," he said, as he stumbled off the slide. "I'm exhausted. I'll have to go to bed early, just like a baby pony. I won't call anything a flapdoodle *ever* again."

"You will," laughed Baby Lucky. "You've won first prize in our all-day sliding marathon, you didn't fall over once. Baby Ribbon made this rosette and I've decided to call it 'Fireball's Flapdoodle'. Let me tie it on for you, Fireball."

Fireball snorted crossly as everyone laughed. Then he started to laugh, too. "All right, call it a flapdoodle," he said. "But I've got a better one for you. Because all the baby ponies are too young to take part in the all-night jumping marathon and because this big boy pony is too tired to take part, I'm going to tell you all an exciting adventure story before we go to bed. And what do you think I'll call it?"

"FIREBALL'S FLAP-DOODLE!" shouted all the baby ponies.

"That's what I'll call my spell," said Kelpy proudly. "Fireball's Flapdoodle. The best spell I've ever made."

"And in the morning, we'll tell you if there were any flapdoodles at our marathon," the mountain ponies promised Fireball as they hurried away. "Don't frighten yourself with your adventure story, Fireball."

"Flapdoodle! As if I would," he laughed. Kelpy looked thoughtful. She'd just remembered a frightening spell...

PONY LAND THROUGH THE YEAR

January

The January bells are ringing,
New Year has just begun!
The little ponies and their friends
Know they'll have a lot of fun.

February

Heart Throb likes February,
Because on Valentine's Day,
Her special friends, the love birds,
Are sure to come and play.

March

The March winds are blowing
And Skyflier shouts with glee,
"Come along, little ponies,
And fly some kites with me!"

April

Princess Pearl likes this month
With all its April showers.
The rain looks just like teardrops,
She watches it for hours.

35

May

Look at all the ribbons
Hanging from the cherry tree.
"I've made a maypole," Bow Tie crie
"Who'll come and dance with me?"

June

In June it's Rosedust's birthday
And the little ponies go
To a party in Flutter Valley,
Where the prettiest flowers grow.

July

In the month of July
There's always a Pony Parade.
And Fizzy makes her special drinks
With ice-cream and lemonade.

August

"It's August!" shouts Baby Lucky.
"We're going to swim in the sea,
I hope the baby sea ponies
Will play all day with me."

37

ptember

September is the time for fruit,
Guess where Applejack will be?
Down in the Pony Land orchard
Collecting apples for her tea.

October

Look at the October leaves
Merrily swirling around.
The little ponies try to catch them
Before they touch the ground.

November

November is cold and foggy
But Princess Amber lights the way,
So the baby ponies and their pals
Can still go out to play.

December

"It's December," laughs Masquerade.
"What a busy month it will be.
I'll have to make a good disguise,
I'm Pony Christmas, you see."

INCESS AMETHYST AND HE DISMAL DANDELIONS

"Baby Lucky!" exclaimed Trickles in dismay. "Whatever have you been doing? You're covered in mud. The Flower Lady will be here any minute, there's no time to take you to the Waterfall for a bubble bath. Oh dear, you know we promised Majesty that we would all look our very best for our visitor."

Just then, Spike ran into the courtyard. He was carrying a bucket of bubbly water and a sponge. "It's all right, Trickles," he panted. "I'll get Baby Lucky clean. After all, it's my fault he's muddy."

"It isn't your fault," denied the baby pony. "It's Princess Amethyst's fault."

"Heavy hooves," groaned Trickles. "Ever since the Princess ponies came to live here, Princess Amethyst has caused more trouble than anyone else."

"She doesn't mean to," said Spike, as he started to rub Baby Lucky's front legs. "She just thinks everybody needs helping all the time. And she just loves to help them."

Spike was speaking the truth. Princess Amethyst loved to help her friends, even when

they didn't need helping. The trouble was, whenever the Princess pony thought about doing a kind deed a bunch of flowers would appear! Then she would worry herself, and her friends, until the flowers had been given back to their rightful owner. Unfortunately, the little ponies often didn't know who the rightful owner was.

"It's Princess Amethyst's fault we've got to look our best for the Flower Lady," snorted Baby Lucky, who didn't like having to stay neat and tidy.

"If she hadn't been in such a helpful mood yesterday, we wouldn't be having this special party for the Flower Lady today."

"That's true," said Trickles, "but we must show her how sorry we are for spoiling her Flower Show."

"We didn't make all those bunches of flowers float out of their vases and come all the way here. Princess Amethyst did that!" retorted Baby Lucky.

"I don't know what you're complaining about, Baby Lucky," said Spike. "You like parties, you know you do."

"But I don't like being washed for them," said the baby pony. "And this is the second wash I've had today." Baby Lucky wriggled impatiently and, somehow, he managed to knock the bucket over.

"Roaring dragons!" shouted Spike. "You aren't anywhere near clean yet and the water has all gone now."

"Never mind," said Trickles, trying not to laugh. She kicked her heels twice and two magic watering cans appeared. "They're full of water and they won't empty until I tell them to," she said.

"I'll tell you the next bit," said Baby Lucky. "Spike shouted at me to run. I ran so fast that I couldn't see where I was going..."

"He tripped over a twig and fell into that muddy patch where Lemon Drop made her obstacle course," laughed Spike. "He did look funny!"

"It wasn't funny!" Baby Lucky glared at his friend.

"It was," said the little dragon. "Your front legs went up in the air, then your back legs slipped, you landed on your back...then...then you rolled over and made your front all muddy."

"You wouldn't think it was so funny if *you* had to have two washes," said Baby Lucky. "I'll show you what I mean." He was just about to snatch the watering can out of Spike's paws when Trickles kicked her heels twice and the watering cans disappeared.

"You're clean now, Baby Lucky," said Trickles. "And listen! The Flower Lady must be here. Wind Whistler and Medley are playing the tune they made up to welcome her."

"We'd better hurry down to the meadow," suggested

"Come on, Spike, we'll have a watering can each and you can tell me how Baby Lucky got so muddy while we're cleaning him."

"Well, I was standing on Baby Lucky's back to reach a plum from the tree," explained the little dragon. "It was a nice big juicy plum. We wanted it to give to the Flower Lady at teatime. Anyway, I was just about to pick it when I saw Princess Amethyst coming through the orchard. I didn't want her to see us and think we needed helping, so I..."

Spike. "That's where we're having the party."

"We'll hurry but we won't run," laughed Baby Lucky. "I don't want to fall in any more mud!"

"Where have you been?" asked Majesty, when Spike, Trickles and Baby Lucky hurried into the meadow. "Everybody else is here."

"I was having another..." began Baby Lucky, but Spike interrupted him.

"Shh!" said the little dragon. "Princess Amethyst is about to make her speech, she's walking onto the platform."

The Princess pony bowed regally then looked down towards the Flower Lady who was sitting in the seat of honour. "This party is a very special one," said Princess Amethyst. "It's to show our friend the Flower Lady how sorry I am for spoiling her Flower Show. I'd like to..." Princess Amethyst stopped talking and stared in dismay at the Flower Lady.

There was a big, furry caterpillar crawling over the Flower Lady's bonnet. The caterpillar was the Flower Lady's pet, but Princess

Amethyst didn't know that. "I must help her, somehow," whispered the Princess pony to herself. "I'll have to..."

However, before Princess Amethyst had time to think what she could do about the furry caterpillar, an enormous bunch of enormous dandelions landed in the Flower Lady's lap!

"Weeping willow!" exclaimed the Flower Lady. "These dandelions are from Leander's Clock Tower. We must take them back, or...or..." The Flower Lady covered her face with her hands.

"Or what?" demanded Princess Aquamarine, who was standing next to the Flower Lady. "And *who* is Leander? What a lovely name, I think he must be a handsome prince. He's waiting for..." The Princess pony's eyes took on a dreamy look.

"Aquamarine!" Princess Sapphire, the wise Princess pony, spoke sharply. "Aquamarine, don't you dare get your head in a cloud. Stop dreaming this instant. I think we're in trouble."

"Oh, we are, we are," moaned the Flower Lady. "Leander is a Lion Man. He's very quiet and very kind as long as the dandelions are guarding the Clock Tower he lives in. But if the dandelions aren't there, he will think it's time for him to be as brave as a lion and go into battle. He's got a silver sword and he just needs to point it at someone or something and whatever he's pointing it at falls down and can't ever get up again."

"Where is the Clock Tower?" shouted the little ponies, who had gathered around the Flower Lady. "We *must* take the dandelions back."

"That's the trouble," sighed the Flower Lady. "The Clock Tower moves from place to place. I don't know where it is at this moment."

Just then, the furry caterpillar jumped from the Flower Lady's bonnet into the enormous bunch of dandelions. "Furry-Foot," said the Flower Lady to the caterpillar. "Can you help us, my pretty pet. Do you know where the Clock Tower is?"

"Pathetic Princess," whispered Princess Amethyst to herself. "The Flower Lady didn't need help after all. The caterpillar is her friend!"

Furry-Foot wriggled busily amongst the enormous dandelions. "Her eyes are moving round and round," whispered the Flower Lady, looking down at her pet. "That means the dandelions are telling her something."

The caterpillar jumped onto the Flower Lady's hand. "They won't tell me where the Clock Tower is," she reported. "They don't ever want to go back there. It's so dismal for them, you see. They have to keep perfectly still and straight all the time. If just one dandelion moves the slightest bit, Leander thinks there's an enemy coming."

"I sneezed one day," said one of the dandelions, in a slow, dismal voice. "Leander dashed for his silver sword,

pointed it at a stone statue and the statue fell down. We felt more dismal than ever after that, it used to be such a pretty statue.''

"We want to be like other flowers,'' explained another dismal dandelion. "We want to sway in the breeze and smile in the sun. We want...''

"Listen!'' Majesty spoke urgently. "I can hear the sound of roaring. I think Leander's discovered that the dandelions have gone.''

"We must do something!''

shouted Baby Lucky. "I don't want to fall down and never get up again. We must find out where the Clock Tower is and take the dandelions back.''

"We don't ever want to go back,'' said the dandelions.

"That's no problem, no problem at all,'' stated Princess Amber. Everybody looked hopefully at the Princess pony. She often found a way to solve problems. Maybe she could solve this one. "Majesty,'' continued Princess Amber, "will you twirl your magic horn and make time stand still for Leander?''

Majesty did as Princess Amber asked and the little ponies, the Flower Lady, Furry-Foot and the dismal dandelions waited anxiously to hear what Princess Amber had to suggest.

''Now, all we have to do,'' smiled Princess Amber, ''is to paint a picture of dandelions on the walls of the Clock Tower. Painted dandelions won't move at all!''

''So Leander will never think it's time for him to be as brave as a lion,'' said the Flower Lady. ''What a clever idea. Who'll paint the picture?''

''Princess Amethyst, of course, she's a very good artist,'' said Majesty. The little ponies watched as Majesty twirled her magic horn again.

''Oh, I'm wearing my painting outfit and all my equipment is here,'' laughed Princess Amethyst. ''But now we need to know where the Clock Tower is.''

''We'll tell you now,'' said the dismal dandelions. ''Now we know we won't have to go back and guard it. It's by the Waterfall.''

Trickles kicked her heels twice and two watering cans appeared. ''We'll have to take you with us,'' she told the dandelions. ''Princess Amethyst will need to look at you to make sure the dandelions on the Clock Tower look just like you.''

So Spike and the Flower Lady put the dandelions into the watering cans and everybody hurried to the Waterfall.

''Look, there's Leander,'' said the Flower Lady, as they arrived in the meadow by the

Waterfall. "What a good job you made time stand still for him, Majesty. He was just about to point his silver sword at the Waterfall!"

"And there's the Clock Tower!" shouted Baby Lucky. "Isn't it strange, it's got all sorts of different clocks on it."

"That's so Leander always knows the time," explained the dandelions. "He looks at the clocks and asks if it's time for him to be as brave as a lion. Then, he used to look at us to make sure we were standing still and straight..."

"Well, he'll look at these dandelions now," said Princess Amethyst, painting busily. "And it will never be time for him to be as brave as a lion."

"I wonder what Leander will say if he ever finds out that his dandelion guards were painted by a Princess?" said Princess Aquamarine dreamily.

"There, I've finished," stated Princess Amethyst. She bowed to Majesty, then giggled. "The clocks say that it's time to wake Leander from the spell," she said.

Majesty muttered a few magic words and everybody

watched Leander.

"Ah, visitors!" he cried. "Is it time for me to be as brave as a lion?" He ran over to the Clock Tower and looked at the painted dandelions.

"My guards are standing still and straight," he said. "You must be friends, not enemies."

"We are friends!" shouted Spike, who thought the Lion Man looked almost as brave as a hundred dragons! "We are friends and we've come to invite you to a party."

The party was a huge success. Leander asked if he could stay by the Waterfall, in his Clock Tower, so that he'd be near all his new friends.

And before she went home, the Flower Lady whispered to Princess Amethyst, "I am glad you spoilt my Flower Show yesterday. If you hadn't given this special party for me, the dismal dandelions might never have been freed. Now I'm taking them to live in my garden and they'll never be dismal again." The Flower Lady picked up the two magic watering cans. "I'll carry them home in these," she said.

Princess Amethyst looked thoughtful as the Flower Lady walked away. "No, no," she told herself. "The Flower Lady can manage on her own. She doesn't need any help. Not this time, anyway!"

COTTON CANDY'S CLAY

Hello,
Flowers always seem to be getting Princess Amethyst and me into trouble, don't they? Heavy hooves! These flowers look good enough to eat, but they're made out of clay. I'll tell you how to make the clay then you can design all sorts of scenery to put in your own Pony Land.

You need: 1 cup of flour, $\frac{1}{4}$ cup of salt, $\frac{1}{3}$ cup of water, a wooden spoon and a mixing bowl.

1. Put the flour, salt and water into the mixing bowl.
2. Using the wooden spoon, mix everything up until there aren't any lumps and your clay feels nice and smooth. If it feels crumbly, add a few more drops of water. If it feels runny, add a bit more flour.
3. Now look at all the pictures to see what you can model with your clay. When your models are dry, you can paint them with any water-based paint. When the paint is dry, brush on a coat of clear nail varnish to make your models shine.

GINGERBREAD'S GINGERBREAD JOKE

"You will make the gingerbread men look really special, won't you, Gingerbread?" asked Princess Ruby anxiously.

"It's the very first time that Prince High and Mighty has been to Pony Land. I want everything to be perfect."

"My gingerbread men are always perfect!" replied Gingerbread. "Look, I'm going to decorate them with paper crowns and..."

"You can't use these crowns!" interrupted Princess Ruby. "They're funny. Prince High and Mighty is *very* stand-offish. He'll think we're silly." "Ooh, did you hear that?" whispered Baby Shady, who was just coming into the kitchen with Baby Applejack.

52

"She said our crowns were silly," said Baby Applejack. "And we spent all morning making them."

"I didn't say that! I said Prince High and Mighty will think *we're* silly."

Princess Ruby tossed her mane. "I suggest you make gold crowns," she said, and walked regally from the room. "Heavy hooves! She's gone high and mighty now," snorted Gingerbread.

"I don't think we're going to like Prince High and Mighty," sighed Baby Applejack. "Why is he visiting us, anyway?"

Baby Shady giggled. "He's going to show us how to be high and mighty, like this!" The baby pony jumped onto a table.

"Prince High and Mighty is Prince Faraway's brother," explained Gingerbread, laughing at Baby Shady. "Prince Faraway wants him to meet his friends, especially the Princess ponies." "They used to live in Dismal Desert with Prince Faraway," remembered Baby Applejack.

"I've brought some gold crowns," said Princess Ruby, and she put a box on the table.

"I'm sorry we can't use your crowns," she told the baby ponies. "They just won't do."

"Ours are too funny, ours aren't regal," chanted Baby Shady, dancing on the table. "And you're not to do or say silly things while Prince High and Mighty's here," ordered the Princess pony. "Maybe the baby ponies shouldn't come to tea," she added. "They'll behave," promised Gingerbread.

"We'll be good," agreed Baby Applejack. "I'll put these gold crowns on the gingerbread men. They're very nice."

"You go and get ready, Princess Ruby," said Baby Shady, jumping off the table. "You've got some knots in your mane!"

"Gingerbread, you've got a plan, haven't you?" asked Baby Applejack when the Princess pony had gone. "I saw your eyes twinkling."

"Do you remember those cherry sweets I made?" asked Gingerbread. "The ones that squeaked when you chewed them? Well, I'm..."

"You're going to make some more," giggled the baby ponies. "Can we help?" "Yes, move the biscuits to another table, and we'll make some squeaky cherry buttons to decorate them with," said Gingerbread. "When Prince High and Mighty eats the gingerbread men, we'll pretend they're alive!"

"Just try one of these," said Gingerbread after a while. "I want to make sure they're squeaky enough." The baby ponies chewed a cherry sweet and laughed with delight at the loud noise they made. "Right, put the sweets onto the gingerbread men," smiled Gingerbread.

"You'd better get ready now," said Gingerbread. "Are you going to wear your party dresses?" But just then...

The door opened and Megan came in. "Surprise came to fetch me," she said. "Who's the important visitor you're expecting?"

"Have a gingerbread man," said Gingerbread mischievously, "and we'll tell you all about him." How the ponies laughed when Megan started to eat the squeaky cherry buttons. Then they told her all about their plan for Prince High and Mighty. Megan had a plan, too!

"Shh! Here's Princess Ruby," whispered Gingerbread. "Megan," said the Princess pony, "I am glad you're here."

"Why?" asked Baby Shady. "Megan is always sensible...and do take those silly crowns off, Baby Shady." Megan hid a smile.

"You haven't got your party dresses on," said the Princess pony. "You'll have to come as you are. Hurry, he's here."

Princess Ruby chattered all the way to the throne room. "I hope I get a chance to tell the story," Megan whispered.

"And what do you do when you come to Pony Land?" Prince High and Mighty asked Megan, after Princess Ruby had introduced them. Megan smiled shyly at the arrogant looking prince. "I often tell the little ponies stories," she said. "Perhaps you would like to hear one before tea?"

Megan's plan was working perfectly! She told the story about a gingerbread man. When she got to the part where the gingerbread man was eaten, Princess Pearl began to cry. ''Oh, I love sad stories,'' she sobbed. Baby Applejack smiled happily as she caught a teardrop.

''I hope you don't think I'm rude,'' said the prince. ''But that was a silly story. As if a biscuit could come to life!''

''We're having gingerbread biscuits for tea,'' laughed Gingerbread. ''Come and help me get them, Baby Applejack.''

''I'll come and help, too,'' said Baby Shady. ''I must say, those baby ponies are very polite,'' Prince High and Mighty said approvingly.

''I thought Pony Land might be a rather silly place,'' he added, ''where everybody laughed all the time. I can see I was wrong.''

Later, Prince High and Mighty was enjoying his tea in the banquet hall. He admired the golden crowns on the gingerbread men. "These biscuits aren't alive," said Baby Applejack, politely passing the plate to the prince. The prince started to eat. Squeak-squeak went the cherries.

"Oh dear, that biscuit is alive! Have another one," said Baby Applejack. Then she touched the knot on her handkerchief.

Suddenly, the biscuit wriggled out of the prince's hand. Then it danced over the table! The prince was astounded!

Then he roared with laughter. He laughed and laughed and laughed. "How did you make that happen?" he demanded. Baby Applejack showed him the pearl in her handkerchief. "A wishing pearl from Princess Pearl's tears," she said. "I wished the biscuit alive to see what you'd do." "Thank you," said the prince. "You've reminded me how to enjoy myself."

LOST IN LULLABY NURSERY

The baby ponies are all dressed up in their favourite outfits. But they've lost their pocket pals somewhere in Lullaby Nursery. Can *you* find the twelve pocket pals?